CABO & CORAL GO SURFING!

by
Udo Wahn & Jami Lyn

Copyright © 2007, 2008 by Jami Lyn and Udo Wahn
Library of Congress Control Number: 2006910221
ISBN: 978-0-615-17598-0
eBook ISBN: 978-0 -9833841-0-6
2nd Edition

This is a work of fiction. Names, characters, places and incidents either are the product
of the author's imagination or are used fictitiously, and any resemblence to any actual
persons, living or dead, events, or locales is entirely coincidental.

This book was printed in Singapore by Craft Print International Ltd.

Art Production: Hang 5 Art & Graphics
www.hang5art.com

To order additional copies of this book, contact:
Udo Wahn
udo@caboandcoral.com
www.caboandcoral.com

Dedications

Preface

"Aloha" means more than merely hello and goodbye. It is a value, one of unconditional love and sharing. The "Aloha Spirit" embodies a life full of joy and happiness. When you live aloha, you are living in harmony with others and your environment.

Surfing is a way of life that is best when shared with others. There is nothing as relaxing and cleansing as a surf session with friends. Surfing benefits your overall health and well-being by promoting a fit body and a healthy mind.

With this book we set out to create something that would also be enjoyable for those of you who are parents as they read to their children. We want to take you and your children far from your daily concerns to an idyllic seaside location.

This book is for the next generation of surfers. We hope to teach respect for the ocean with its playful creatures, the beach, and other surfers. Most of all we hope that you and your family will capture the essence of the "Aloha Spirit" and practice it each day!

Introduction

Cabo and Coral are neighbors living near the beach. They went to swim class together when they were toddlers. Now that they are good swimmers, they are ready for the challenge of surfing in our beautiful ocean and making new friends while doing so! They start out with a dawn patrol surf check at their local beach.

Aloha!

"Hey, Cabo! Check out the waves at the point!"

"Coral, the waves at the beach break and reef are looking good too!"

"Cabo, my dad says, 'If in doubt, don't go out!'"

"Let's check with the lifeguards, Cabo, to see if it's okay to surf here."

"Sounds good, Coral. Sometimes only swimmers are allowed in this area."

8

"Cabo, let's put on our sunscreen and rash guards."

"That's a good idea, Coral. We don't want to get sunburned."

9

"This rip current is strong enough to carry us out to the waves, Cabo. But when we are swimming we need to swim along the shore to get out of the rip!"

12

13

15

16

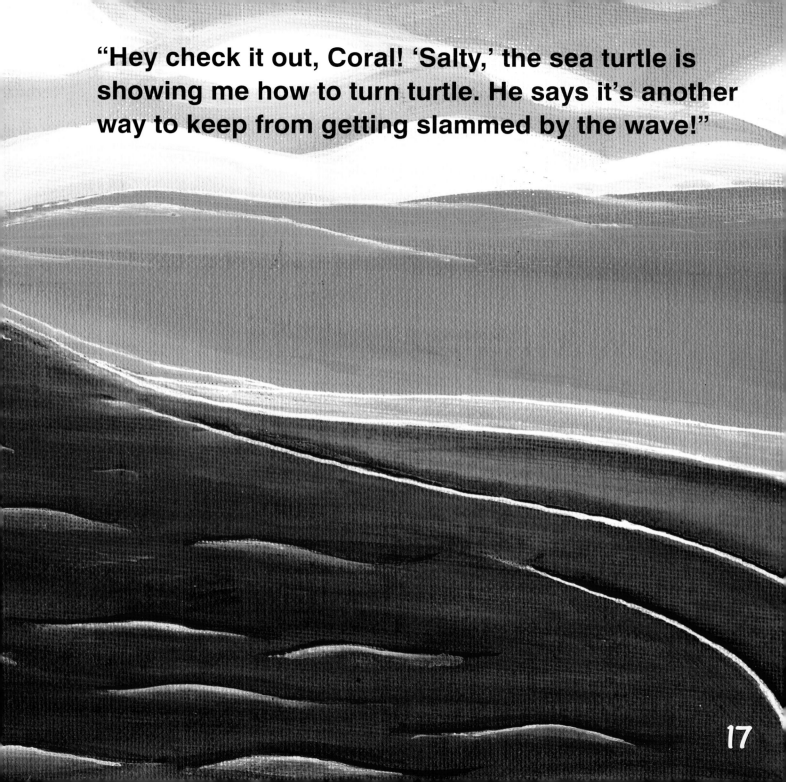

"Hey check it out, Coral! 'Salty,' the sea turtle is showing me how to turn turtle. He says it's another way to keep from getting slammed by the wave!"

"Coral, I could wait for waves all day with all these cool marine animals in the water."

"Me too, Cabo. I feel like I'm a part of nature."

19

"Wow, Coral! I'm flying down the line and really learning how to go for it! It's an awesome feeling."

20

21

22

"Wait your turn, Coral! You're not supposed to cut me off. There are always more waves on the way!"

"Surfing is a challenge for me, Cabo, especially when I am surfing by the pier."

24

25

"Hey Coral! Check out this new trick!
I'm smacking it off the lip!"

"Cabo, it sure is fun sharing waves
with the new friends we made today!
Aloha, friends!"

29

"Wow! Coral, I love getting covered by the wave!"

31

"Coral, thanks for bringing the fruit,
granola bars, juice, and water.
Yummmm, they taste great; plus they're healthy!"

33

"Coral, let's recycle our cans and plastic bottles by putting them in those recycle bins before we go back out surfing."

"Look Cabo! There's some rubbish that someone has left on the beach. Let's clean that up too! If everyone picks up three, what a difference we will see."

37

"Cabo, I'll go left on this wave!"

"Okay, Coral. Then I'll go right, so we can both ride the same wave!"

39

"Come on over here Coral and try this!
It's way more fun to hang five than
play video games! Yahoo!"

41

42

"Look, Cabo! The dolphins are surfing on the wave with us! Wow! How cool is that?"

"Cabo, that was a great day of surfing!
I am so happy! Just look at that sunset!"

"Coral, I can't wait to go surfing again tomorrow."

"Aloha Cabo."

"Aloha Coral."

45

About Jami Lyn

Jami Lyn is a muralist in San Diego, California. She mirrored her artist mother and remembers as a child when the kitchen table was covered with more paint than food! Many of her accomplishments can be seen on her website at jamilynart.com.

About Udo

Udo lives in Del Mar, California where one can usually find him surfing the local reef breaks at 8th, 11th or 15th Street.
Udo often drives deep into remote Baja, Mexico on surf safaris. He has surfed the beaches of Australia, Costa Rica, southwestern France, Mexico, and Hawaii.
He is married to Aleida, and they have a young son, Paolo Cabo.

Aleida and Paolo

Udo's son, Paolo "Cabo" Wahn, and wife, Aleida. The photo of Aleida as a child was the inspiration for "Coral."

Acknowledgements

Rick Doyle a professional surf photographer and videographer for his uplifting comments that encouraged us to complete this book. Learn more about Rick's photography and surf movies at Rick Doyle.com.

Brian Galt, my dear friend and surfing buddy, for his computer graphic skills in preparing the manuscript for publication. His company is Hang 5 Art & Graphics.

Michael Willis, extreme big wave surfing world champion, for his strong support.

Nathan Myers, assistant editor at SURFING magazine for his positive comments about the book and help with locating the migratory pro surfers that we would approach for endorsements!

Kristi Nystul, former assistant art director SURFING magazine for her help with contacting the pro surfers so we could obtain their opinions about the book.

Cobi Emery, founder of pickup3.org, dedicated to cleaning up our beaches.

Carol and Shawn Holder, owners of the Panniken coffeehouse in Leucadia, California for providing an inspirational environment for our collaboration.

Bridget Poizner, founder of Save Their Story Inc. who helped dot the i's and cross the t's.

Our families for their patience, suggestions, and support while we created this book for the next generation of surfers.

Visit us at **www.cabandcoral.com**

Surfrider Foundation®

Each year over 18,000 beaches across the United States are closed or posted as unhealthy. If we all pitch in, we can make a difference in working to keep our coastal waters and beaches clean and healthy.

*Here are some recommendations provided by the **Surfrider Foundation** that you, your friends and family can do to help our beaches:

1. Pick up pet poo. Pet poo that reaches the ocean can make both people and animals sick!
2. Rake and bag your yard clippings. Grass and yard clippings that get blown into the street often end up in the ocean, making it a place for harmful bacteria to grow.
3. It's best not to smoke. But if someone you know does smoke, make sure they put the cigarette out and toss it in the correct container. Cigarette butts make up much of the trash on the beach! Yuck!
4. Don't hose down your driveways. Not only does it waste water, but it causes oils and other icky stuff to end up in our oceans. Use a broom instead.
5. Plant gardens with plants that do not need much water. Those kinds of plants help keep our beaches clean.
6. Always dispose of used motor oil properly. Never dump it in a storm drain or field. Take it to a gas station or the dump for recycling.
7. When you go to the beach, make sure you not only pick up your trash, but try and pick up at least one piece of somebody else's. If everyone did this, our beaches and coastlines would get better real quick! Yahoo!
8. Ask your parents to cut back on fertilizers. Excess fertilizer gets into our oceans and streams and can cause harmful plankton blooms, or red tides, which harm fish, dolphins and other sea life.

Another great thing you and your family can do is join the Surfrider Foundation. They are a non-profit grassroots environmental organization that works to protect oceans, waves and beaches. They have over 60 chapters across the country that are made up of people just like you and me, who all get together and do beach clean-ups, water testing and other activities.

* Modification of a **Surfrider** original.